Rumpelstiltskin

Retold by Susanna Davidson

Illustrated by
Desideria Guicciardini

Reading Consultant: Alison Kelly
Roehampton University

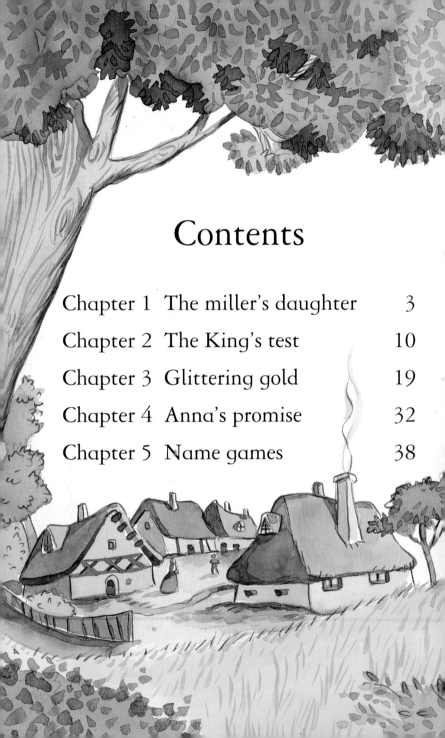

Contents

Chapter 1   The miller's daughter   3

Chapter 2   The King's test   10

Chapter 3   Glittering gold   19

Chapter 4   Anna's promise   32

Chapter 5   Name games   38

Chapter 1

The miller's daughter

Once upon a time there was a poor miller, who loved to show off. He boasted about *everything*.

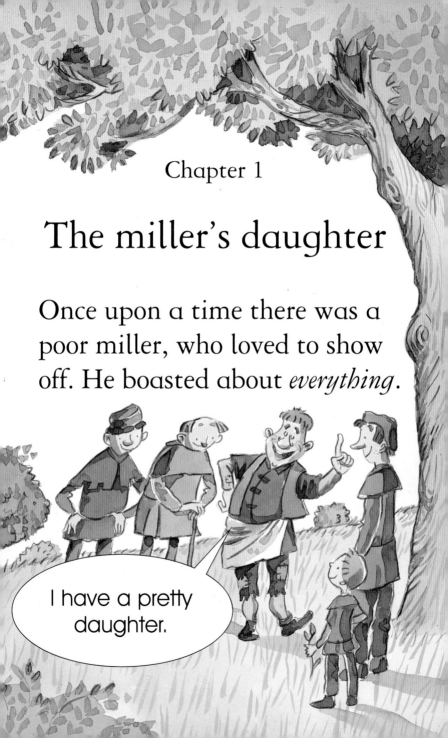

I have a pretty daughter.

Sometimes his boasts were true...

Hello, Father.

and sometimes they weren't...

I'm the best looking man around.

One day, on his way back
from a hunt, the King rode
through the miller's village.
Suddenly, he stopped.

A beautiful girl was
standing on the path.

"What's your name?" asked the King, gazing at her.

"Her name is Anna," said the miller, quickly. "She's my daughter...

...and she can spin straw into gold," he added, boasting as usual.

"Really?" asked the King. "Yes, really," replied the miller, nodding his head.

"In that case, bring her to my castle," ordered the King, and rode away.

7

"This is your chance, Anna," cried the miller. "The more the King sees your pretty face, the more he'll want to marry you. You could be Queen!"

The next morning, the miller took Anna to see the King.

The castle walls were old and crumbling. Windows were broken and doors were missing.

"The King must be short of money," whispered the miller.

"You can go!" the King commanded the miller. "As for you," he said, turning to Anna, "follow me."

Chapter 2

The King's test

The King led Anna down dark corridors and up twisting stairs. At last they reached a tiny room, stuffed with straw.

10

In the corner was a large spinning-wheel. "You're pretty enough to marry," said the King. "But are you as clever as your father says?"

"You have tonight to turn this straw into gold. If you fail, you shall die." Then he went out and locked the door.

Anna sat down, put her head in her hands and sobbed. "Oh Father!" she cried. "What have you done?"

I don't want to die!

"I want to be Queen, but I can't spin straw into gold. No one can!"

12

"That's what you think!"
came a voice from
the window.

Anna jumped. There, by the
window, was a little man —
riding on a wooden spoon.

His long white beard
waved about in the wind.
"Hurry up," he shouted,
"and let me in!"

It's cold
out here!

With a trembling
hand, Anna opened
the window...

...and the little man flew in.

"Mistress Miller," he said
with a smile. "What will you
give me if I spin that straw
into gold?"

For a moment, Anna
was too shocked to speak.
She could only open and
close her mouth,
like a fish.

"I c-c-could give you my
necklace?" she said, at last.
"Perfect," said the little man,
grabbing it.

He leaped onto the stool,
tossed his beard over his
shoulder and began to spin.

whirr whirr whirr

Anna gasped in surprise. The
straw was changing into gold
before her eyes.

17

She tried to see how it was done. But as she watched the whirring wheel, she felt her eyes begin to close.

Soon, she was fast asleep.

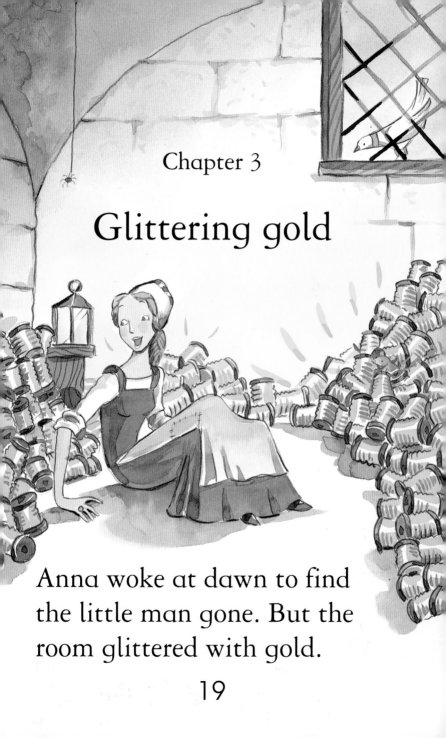

Chapter 3

Glittering gold

Anna woke at dawn to find the little man gone. But the room glittered with gold.

When the King came in, his eyes lit up in delight. "But it's not enough for me," he said. "I need you to spin *more* gold."

I have servants to pay...

He took Anna to a second room, larger than the one before.

Once again, it was stuffed with straw.

"You have tonight to turn this straw to gold. If you fail, you shall die," said the King.

Then he went out,
and locked the door.

Anna sat on the stool
and cried. "I still don't
know how to spin straw
into gold," she sobbed.

22

But that night, the little
man came again.

"What will you give me if I
spin this time?" he asked.

"I'll give you the ring on my
finger," Anna replied.

"Perfect," said the little
man. He pulled off her ring,
hung his beard over his ears
and began to spin.

Whirr whirr whirr

whirr, whirr, whirr went
the wheel, all through the
night. The little man left as
the sun rose.

24

When the King came in, he jumped for joy. "But I still need more gold!" he cried.

"After all, I've a country to run and enemies to fight. I want enough money to last my whole life."

He took Anna to another room, even larger than the one before. This one was bursting with great piles of straw.

"You must spin this too, all through the night. And if you succeed, you shall be my wife."

That night, the little man appeared for the third time. "What can you give me now, Mistress Miller?" he asked.

"Oh!" cried Anna. "I have nothing left to give."

27

"Then promise me your first born child," said the little man. "And if I refuse?" asked Anna.

"I won't spin," he snapped. Anna thought for a while. "I *do* want to be Queen... and he might forget his request..."

Finally she said, "I promise."
The little man grinned, tied
his beard under his chin and
began to spin.

The next morning, the King
was dazzled by all the gold.
"At last!" he cried. "I have all
the gold I'll ever need."

"Anna," he said, "you are
both beautiful *and* clever.
Will you marry me?"

"Oh yes!" said Anna, at once. And so Anna, the poor miller's daughter, became Queen.

Chapter 4

Anna's promise

A year later, Anna gave birth
to a beautiful boy. She loved
him more than her own life.

But, one dark winter's day, the Queen heard a tapping noise at her window.

Let me in!

"Oh no!" she gasped. "The little man's back!"

"You can't come in!" cried the Queen, clutching her baby.

"That's what you think," said the little man.

He disappeared from the window. The Queen waited. "Perhaps he's gone?" she hoped.

The next moment, there
was a rustling noise in
the chimney and the
little man *whooshed*
into the room.

"Give me the
baby, as you
promised," he cried,
dancing around
the room.

"Take whatever you want," pleaded the Queen. "You can have all my money and all my jewels. But please let me keep my son."

"No!" said the man. "Something alive means more to me than all the treasures in the world."

The Queen wept and begged and wept again. At last, the little man took pity on her.

"I will give you three days," he said. "If you can find out my name before then, you may keep the child."

Chapter 5

Name games

The Queen lay awake through the night, trying to remember every name she had ever heard.

When the little man came
the next evening, the Queen
recited all the names she knew.
"Is it James, Peter, John..."
she began.

But to every one, the little
man shook his head and said,
"That is not my name."

On the second day,
the Queen rode far
and wide, asking
everyone their names.

That night, she recalled the
strange new names. "Is your
name Sheepshanks, Shortribs,
Laceleg..?" she asked.

But to every one, the little man shook his head and said, "That is not my name."

You'll never guess!

By the third day, the Queen was in despair. She sat down for supper with the King, but could hardly eat a thing.

"I have a strange tale to tell you," said the King. "Two days ago I went hunting through a deep, dark forest. In the middle of the forest was a little house."

"Outside the house, the strangest little man was jumping about. He hopped on one leg and sang..."

Today I bake, tomorrow brew,

The next I'll do the same.

Ha! Glad I am that no one knew

That **Rumpelstiltskin** is my name.

The Queen smiled when
she heard the King's story,
but she didn't say a word.

When the little
man arrived that night he said,
"Well, Mistress Queen, do you
know my name?"

At first the Queen said,
"Is your name Solomon?"
"No," said the little
man, jumping up and
down in excitement.

"Is your name Zebedee?"
"No," said the little man,
leaping around the room.

45

"Perhaps," said the Queen, after a long pause, "perhaps, your name is Rumpelstiltskin?"

"How did you know that?
How did you know that?"
cried the little man.

With a roar, Rumpelstiltskin jumped on his spoon and shot through the wall.

He was never seen again.

The tale of *Rumpelstiltskin* was first written down by Jacob and Wilhelm Grimm, in Germany, in 1812. There are lots of different versions of the story. In some, Rumpelstiltskin runs away at the end. In others, he flies away on a spoon. In the Grimms' last version, Rumpelstiltskin is so angry, he tears himself in two.

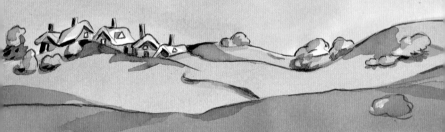

Series editor: Lesley Sims
Designed by Louise Flutter

First published in 2006 by Usborne Publishing Ltd., Usborne House, 83-85 Saffron Hill, London EC1N 8RT, England. www.usborne.com
Copyright © 2006 Usborne Publishing Ltd.